Call The Wolf

Ginny Thomas

Contents

Chapter One

P ilgrimagE

Charles looked out towards the meadow, savoured the vague breeze on his sticky skin. It was noon. The July-sun had just taken its highest place in the sky and made every plant sulk, as well as caused every waterhole hiding within the forest to condensate. Its inhabitants hadn't seen rain for the better part of the month. The meadow in which Charles' cabin was located within was just as brown and dry as the surrounding treeline, but the man himself looked strikingly alive. His posture was impeccable as he sat perfectly still on the veranda, allowing his eyes to play far past the wooden staircase leading out of the cabin's patio. Each day for two months he'd done the same thing, noted the same thing: electricity sparking in the air. Incidentally, something else was also craving his attention. A second mind was burrowing into his, not delivering any clear wishes but an abstract weariness Charles had come to recognize - its intentions, as well. "No," he responded, very calmly, seemingly addressing the meadow itself. "I cannot return, Kripin. Not yet." This time It was more adamant, wavering Charles' concentration just enough to annoy him. "Step down. I've told you, something is going to happen and I have to be present for it - I trust the pack is well under your leadership." A slight disturbance in the nagging presence made Charles sigh, unnoticeably clench a particular muscle in his jaw. Kripin had already taken too much of his time. With a brisk armoring of his thoughts, Charles shut out the other mind invading his and was once again alone. It was important that he remained so. What he was going through was a pilgrimage each alpha had to experience - one last hinderance to then end up alongside the greats in history. A cleansing of the spirit, far away from the support of ones pack.Each alpha gained something different from it, and each one knew individually when it was time. Some returned after months with a wolf twice as strong as before, some brought luck back upon their packs. Charles had felt the undeniable pull a couple months back and ended up in that particular lonesome cabin, lacking food and water, waiting for something he couldn't identify. But he was nothing if not resilient.Charles steadied his posture, drew a deep breath, and closed his eyes; another day was before him.

Something made the cabin tremble, the porch's beams rattle. Charles' eyes shot open and his being returned to an attentive state after countless hours of floating into mindlessness. He put his hands to the boards, perked his hearing.There it was again, this time followed by a wailing moan.Charles got up, quickly locating the back of the cabin as the source of the ruckus. He allowed his nails to sprout, transform into deadly claws, as he cautiously began rounding the cottage.

He wasn't certain what he had expected to find; perhaps a hostile wolf or a packmember not satisfied with his sudden disappearance. He did know that what he in fact did find wasn't in the realm of what he would consider possible: a human.She laid against the cottage's spotty paint, colored the exposed wood with her own red leaking from multiple wounds. Her body was close to gone but her mind was still fighting, trying to keep herself from slipping into darkness. Her eyes were plastered to the treeline hundred meters away, alert and terrified.She finally noticed Charles and, upon realizing she couldn't run away, forced out a pained, "Please... help."Charles watched her, then the treeline, with narrowed eyes. He slowly neared. "Who did this to you? How did you get here?"She followed his gaze back to the forest and pressed herself further against the cabin. She was a small thing, even for a human. "You cannot let them find me! Please, you cannot."Charles was at this point closer to her than he had been to any human prior. Slightly hesitant, he bent down and sniffed her, but the blood was too much for him to be able to detect any other scents."Please," she repeated. Her hand flew out, gripped his arm and squeezed with the last of her strength. Her awareness was fighting a losing battle and Charles could tell she would faint within the next moments. Her attention was still not on him. "Do not let them get me... They are not who they claim to be."Gone.Charles removed his arm from her limp grasp and stood up. He tried to convince himself to go back up front, to continue his journey before the woman would ruin too much. After all, it wasn't his responsibility to look after every human; they were much too fragile for that to be a possible thing to do.Humans died, and that was that.Charles really couldn't justify why he was soon thereafter carrying the pitiful creature indoors, abandoning his stone-solid routine he'd held for the past two months to tend to her wounds.As he sat by her bedside at the end of the day, watching her chest rise and fall with unsteady hitching and writhing, he attempted to make himself cast her out. Nevertheless, as darkness arrived, she was still sound in his bed, ignorant to the sharp eyes observing her, trying to determine her fate and his part in it."You humans get yourself in all kinds of trouble," Charles thought aloud, letting his chin rest on top his fists. "War, heartbreak, petty squabble." The candlelight danced across her face, highlighted the cuts and bruises splattered across her skin. He once again marvelled at her small, very human frame. She could probably be broken with a single, slightly too tight, grip. Perhaps that could come in handy. "But who could you have offended to this degree?"She didn't respond - obviously.Charles felt dumb. He stood from his chair, blew out the candles, and closed the door as he left the bedroom. Kripin was still at it trying to peck into his head but Charles kept him out, wondering if it was unwise to not mention the human in his bed to his closest in command.He came to the realization that it was, but he didn't feel like explaining himself tonight. He'd had far too much encounters than he was supposed to have during the pilgrimage already. So he sat himself back on the porch, drew a deep breath, and tried to numb the racing thoughts of what could be hiding in the woods - what could be chasing a human.

For the first time in two months, the night wasn't calm for Charles.

A

Chapter Two

F iltH

The sun had risen once again on the desolate cabin. All of the windows were wide open, allowing little breeze to invite the curtains to dance. They jumped in and out past the sill, almost fooling the eye to think they were more than dusty old cloth. In a sense, the cabin looked peaceful; dead, almost.Charles was beginning his fifth consecutive hour of keeping watch of the human in his bed. He sat in a chair situated at the far corner of the room, just the way he liked it, and brooded. By then someone had visited the front door of the cabin thrice, someone in quite the hurry judging by their harsh treatment of the oak wood. Charles hadn't let them in.Now they were back.The knocking hadn't begun yet but he could smell them exiting the treeline; cheap liqour and old sweat. Two of them, both too loud for his already aggrevated state, were definitely readying for a fourth round of assault to the door. This time they wouldn't leave without what they wanted.And Charles suspected he was staring right at her.

Charles got up and exited the bedroom. On his way to the front door he allowed his beast to play just beneath his skin, granting him an advantage should things become violent.He threw open the door at the same time two men stepped onto his porch. He instantly noted the rifles strapped to their backs and closed the door behind him."Oh, well howdy there, fella," one said, clearly caught off guard. Human. He was a scrawny thing, both thin and dirty. In his eyes was a spark telling he held more intelligence than he wanted to share.Charles crossed his arms. Nodded once but nothing more.The thin man forced a laugh and ran his tongue across his teeth. "My name's Buck and this here is Neal - we are the closest thing you have to neighbors, I'm guessin'.""That's the reason you have been assaulting my door since this morning," Charles said shortly.Buck gave another weasel-like laugh and shared a brief look with his partner before tipping his straw-hat. "No, sir. Our business is more... pressing. You see, we work with the police on occasion - missing cases here in the woods and stuff like that. Ain't nobody know these grounds like us."Charles suspected Buck wanted an answer but he didn't supply one, mostly because he enjoyed the uncertain glances exchanged between the two men - they were bordering on fearful."Anyway, there's gone a girl missing right around here," Buck continued, poorly concealing how badly he cared about the case by pausing to spit just below the porch. "The coppers told us she's delusional and if anyone sees her it should be reported instantly.""You're wondering if I've seen her?""Have you?" Neal interjected for the first time, his urgent tone earning a glare from his partner."No," Charles said finally, leaning against the doorframe. "No, I haven't seen anything. If I do I'll make sure to call the... coppers.""No," Buck said a little too quickly. He attempted to downplay his response by scratching his chin, letting his eyes roam the meadow. "No, you can call us instead. We'll take good care of her until the coppers come I promise you. Here, our number's on there."Charles took the extended note with an almost unnoticeable grimace. Filthy."Call us if you see anything. Anything at all. She's delusional, maybe even dangerou s.""I will," he lied and enclosed his fist around the paper, inheretly making Buck frown. "Now I have some coffee waiting for me inside so...""Yes, of course, don't let us disturb you any longer. Thank you for your time, sir."

Charles sighed as he closed the door behind him. He instantly threw the note aside and began making his way back to the bedroom. His mind was so preoccupied with the meeting that he didn't notice how the scent coming from the room housing the human had changed.He entered to a pair of wide eyes."That was them, wasn't it?" the woman asked without wasting any time, holding the sheets close to her chest. Her voice was a ball of fear and broken glass.Charles slowly closed the door. "Two me n.""Dirty, holding rifles?"He nodded. "They claimed to be working with the police."The woman's eyes dimmed as her mind went elsewhere. "That cannot be true," she thought aloud. "You didn't tell them I was here, did you?"Charles sat himself down on the foot of the bed, observed the red stain left on the pillow after the woman's head. "No."She exhaled, leant back against the headboard. She looked endlessly tired. "Thank god.""T hose men, are they the ones who did this to you?"To Charles surprise, the woman laughed slightly. It was a wheezing sound, interrupted by a trail of coughs, but a laugh nonetheless. Hooded eyes fixated him. "What, I'm not pretty anymore?""Until a few minutes ago, I wasn't certain you were alive anymore," he lied. Of course he'd kept close watch of her condition all night and day."I don't die quite that easily," she murmured but couldn't hide how his words affected her. "But thank you, you saved my life."He didn't respond."My name is Sara," she continued on, not deterred by his silence."No it isn't.""No." She looked down to her hands, then back at him. Her eyes looked almost pitch black behind her soiled bangs. "I'm Maria.""Charles.""I-is there something wrong?"He hadn't even realized he was grimacing before she commented on it, but even then he couldn't stop. He put a hand over his mouth and nose and stood up so suddenly it made Maria jump."You smell."She frowned and took a whiff of her armpit before whipping her head to the side as if she could somehow escape her own odor. "Yeah, I do.""You need to wash.""I need to do a lot of things."He ignored her comment and continued, "There is a lake near here, big enough to not have been taken by the heat.""But the men...""They're nothing I can't handle."With a single once-over Maria decided she believed him. But she remained under the covers still. "Don't you want to know why they're after me? Who I am?""I do not want to get involved further. My morals are the only things keeping me from kicking you out. Now come."

Maria threw the covers off in a single swift motion. She watched his reaction closely as she put her feet on the floor. Her eyebrows rose suggestively. "And that's all?""Yes.""Do I have your word? Because if you intend to rape me then I'd like to know."Charles' only response was opening the door. His eyes descended to her trembling legs; the human woman was most likely not as tough as she'd like to be. "You're going to fall if you stand too quickly," he warned. "I don't want to have to bury you so take your time."Maria nodded but didn't seem to know what it entailed to be careful. She began walking much too fast and only managed a couple steps towards the door before falling forward.Charles was immediately there to hold her upright."Thank you," she murmured, each word clearly straining her. Charles began feeling like a child who'd brought in a dying bird. "I'll be better in no time, just have to... stretch my legs a little. Do you have food?""No.""Really?""I'm on a spiritual journey. I do not need food."Maria quieted for a second, fell into his pace as he lead her out the door. She watched him through her bangs. "You're a good man, Charles."

Charles only nodded, didn't bother correcting her despite knowing he wasn't a man - and definitely not good.

A/nLet me know if you liked it!

Chapter Three

C urrentS

Maria moved her fingers. She felt the chilly currents dance around them and tried to not think about the dark void beneath her back. Her lungs tried to get used to the cold water appearing and dissipating across her chest but it was hard and at times she felt her legs sink into the lake's depth.Charles sat on the shoreline, watching her as well as their surroundings. It wasn't sirene; somewhere, Buck and Neal could be hiding, waiting for him to lower his guard.He wouldn't."You've been in there a while."M aria drew a deep breath. "I have. Are you sure you don't want to get in? I can keep watch just as well as you.""I highly doubt that."The otherwise still water bubbled and moved as Maria switched her position. Now, the only part of her not submerged was her head while she paddled to keep herself afloat. She gave a small smile. "There are some rules in life, Charles."Before he could stop himself he raised an eyebrow, giving her everything she needed to continue."For example, one does not pass on the opportunity to bathe in a lake as perfect as this one." "I'm good.""Look!" Seemingly ignoring his answer, Maria drew a deep breath, readying herself for what ever act. Her eyes went into the water with concentration making Charles involved. He hesitantly put a hand to the sand, not sure that she would be able to do too much in her current state.She disappeared, leaving nothing but a few bubbles behind - those soon dissapeared as well."Maria," Charles barked, scanning the water for any sign of her head breaking through the surface. "Maria? Dammit!"

Without much to it, Charles stood up and dove into the water. He let his hands lead the way, searching the bottom as well as the water while on his way up. He broke through the surface with an uncomfortable feeling nipping at his gut."Aha!"Maria drew some exhasparated breaths as she appeared just left of Charles. She removed some hair glued to her forehead and grinned through the water dripping down her lips.She met his disapproving gaze with her own sprite one, still breathing heavily."I got you," she said. "But I have to be honest, I was beginning to get scared too.""That was unwise. And I wasn't scared."Charles glowered into the water, wondering what he was doing. Had she really been in trouble, what was it to him? She was human, and quite an aggravating one.Maria splashed some water in his face, not furthering her case, but as Charles looked up she wasn't smiling anymore - she seemed ashamed, almost."I'm sorry for ruining your spiritual journey."Despite his best efforts, Charles enjoyed the cool water. He laid his head back and, for the first time in too long, let the sweat and dirt wash off. "Mhm."But he still felt Maria's curious gaze on him."What kind of journey is it?" she asked finally, gathering some water in her hands and pouring it over her head. "What's the purpose?""To get stronger.""Really?"Maybe it was the unfamiliar sense of calm that made Charles so compliant because he nodded. "Mentally. It's a rite of passage. My father did it before me and his father before him. I won't be whole until I complete it.""So what are you, some kind of monk?""I agreed to let your secrets rest. Perhaps you could grant me the same favor."Maria nodded, gave him an odd look, and then dipped her head once again, massaging her scalp. Meanwhile, Charles finally rose his head from the water. He shook his hair somewhat dry and drew a deep breath that filled his nose with a stinging stench.Filth.

Charles lowered himself back down, leaving only his eyes visible, narrowed and scouting. As Maria emerged from the depths he quickly made sure she also remained as submerged as possible. He held a hand to her shoulder, nodded once to the shoreline where loud voices were disturbing the cicadas."The bridge," he said shortly, pushing her in the direction of the broken, run-down wooden contraption that once must have belonged to some nearby cottage, now most likely long gone. A small boat was attached to it, joyfully swaying on the water's surface. Other than that it was long forgotten.As quiet as possible, Maria hurried towards it.

"She couldn't have made it this far, I'm telling you!" a familiar, rodent-like voice exclaimed. Two seconds later, Buck appeared on the shore, his boots trampling the stray grass emerging from the sand. He looked around him as if the entire forest disgusted him. "She was too hurt...""Well, then she must have been with that guy," someone, most likely Neal, responded from within the trees."What guy?""The guy in the cabin, he must've lied."Buck hummed thoughtfully but continued towards the water nonetheless. Charles realized he would soon be spotted and decided to take off. His eyes went to the bridge and he was relieved to see Maria perched underneath it, hiding behind some of the more rotten planks half-way devoured by the water. She met his gaze and it was clear she could hear them just as well as him.By the time Buck's boots sunk into the soil, Charles had made it beside Maria."I'm sorry," she whispered. "I thought they were gone.""No, they're not leaving without you, I suspect."Unbeknownst to herself, she touched two fingers to a particularly deep cut on her right cheekbone.Neal joined Buck by the water."Maria, where have you gone..."They watched the lake as if she would suddenly sprout from the calm surface.A few metres away, Maria pulled away from Charles. She hid her face behind a curtain of wet hair and tried to calm her breathing. A familiar metallic taste spread throughout her mouth, made it feel as if though melted copper was running through her veins.Not now.She pressed her nails into her palms, bit down on her tongue - anything to keep her from screaming in pain. Just below her chin, a lone tadpool wiggled its way through the water and she targeted it with obsessive concentration.Someone grabbed her shoulder, making her cry out."Maria," Charles said severely, removing his hand. "They're gone."She looked up to see that he was right, and that he'd noticed her episode, but thankfully wasn't subjected to any questioning."Thank god. Truly, Charles, I didn't know they would come. If I did then--""We have to go. They might come back."She wasn't sure whether he was angry or simply wanted to spare her pride; was she supposed to feel hurt or grateful?"Y-yeah, let's go."

Charles was swift. With little effort he'd exited the bridge's rotten base and was heading for the shore. Maria was left behind, struggling a little more to maneuver around the boards. As she was about to head out into open water, she braved to turn around, look after the tadpool. It took a second but she found it quite easily, floating about.She clenched her fists, looked to make sure Charles was far away, and then quickly shoveled some water onto it to make it disappear.It had been burnt to a crisp.

A/nI'm gonna enter into the Wattys, y'all. Hence the spamming

Chapter Four

O liveS

"Here.""W-what is this?""Food. As you requested."Maria remained in her somewhat laying position on the porch's steps and didn't hide her disgust when looking at the pile of unprocessed meat on the grass in front of her. Flies were buzzing around, fighting for a piece. She waved some away when they got too close."I can't eat that," she said, risking sounding rude.Charles stood above the meat, hands on his hips, wearing clothes still droopy with lake water. He watched the flies as well."I don't understand your aversion. You have to eat to get strong enough to move on."Maria closed her eyes and turned her face back to the sun, feeling the last of the water leave her dress."I know," she countered. "But that will get me sick. It's raw and dirty and, oh, my god, is that a kidney?""Spleen," Charles corrected, looking disgruntled. "And this is all I have. Except perhaps... the underground cellar. I think I saw a few jars down there.""Maybe that's better. Want help?"Charles declined the offer and went on his own. As soon as his steps disappeared into the cabin, Maria sat herself upright. She reached for a piece of meat, the one seeming the most clean, and pressed it between her palms. As far as she could tell, Charles was an excellent hunter and this was all from some kind of storage he kept.But she still didn't trust it.Making sure she was alone, Maria closed her eyes. She allowed what she imagined as a small box she kept within her chest to open. Just a little, enough for her to handle. Power flowed out, seared within her flesh before entering the piece of meat and searing that, too. She allowed herself to enjoy the fire for a second before forcing the heat back where it belongs: deep within.She hurried to eat the piece of meat, trying not to dwell too much on her inner workings.

As Charles returned with a jar of olives in his hand he could sense the smell of cooked flesh but didn't ponder too much. He gave Maria the jar and, though she didn't seem too hungry, she scooped up a few and let them drop into her mouth.She offered him the one's left. He declined."Where is the nearest town?""Far away I suspect. The only one I know of is Vinnar and that is approximately a day's march," he threw his thumb over his shoulder, "that way."Maria sighed. "That doesn't sound too good. But I'll need to leave soon. They could be back any second."There was no need to further explain whom she meant. She held her breath, almost expected him to finally ask what Buck and Neal were to her, but he didn't. Not even close."You should head out some early morning. You don't want to be in these woods after nightfall.""Yeah..." She stretched her legs, felt her toes crack, and yawned. The heat made her feel like a lazy cat, lounging around with its tail loosely flicking away company. But her mind was too stressed. "Know what I plan to do once I get out of here?""No, what?""Everythin g."Her voice changed so suddenly that Charles' eyes momentarily went to her lips. She was smiling, but not at him."I'm going to rent a car - or steal one. Then I'll drive. For as long as I can. I hope to end up on the other side of the earth before I get tired.""You know someone there?""No," she laughed. "That's what makes it so great."He hummed but seemed to be holding something back. Maria noticed. She cocked her head."What about you?" she asked."I have responsibilities that await me once I'm done." He closed his eyes, made a face as if he had a headache nearing. "Actually, they cannot seem to wait even until then.""Do you like it?"He gave her an odd look, a silent question."Whatever it is that you do," she explained."A lot of people rely on me.""And you still haven't answered."Maria gave a cheeky grin before plopping another olive into her mouth. The metallic taste exploded as she bit down, it made her jaw clench. She offered him one. This time he accepted."I think it's going to work out, your soul searching. You're strong.""Mhm."Maria nodded once. Adamant. "I can tell."She gave him another look, ate another olive. She grinned. Black olive skin covered her upper row of teeth and for the first time Charles gave in, a small smile playing in the corner of his mouth. Maria wiped the olive pieces off using her tongue and got to her feet."Well then! I'm heading inside - no, no, you can stay here. I've disturbed your meditation enough I'm guessing."Charles settled himself on the boards as the front door slammed shut behind him. He drew in the afternoon air, thick and heavy, and closed his eyes.But something was poking at his sense of smell. Something strange. He traced it to the jar of olives and carefully picked it up. He narrowed his eyes at the label. Over the faded letters rested a thin layer of something black, something that had made some of the paper turn yellow at the edges: soot.

A/nThis one's shorter but I promise the next one's gonna blow your mind.Let me know if you like the story so far

Chapter Five

I nfernO

Maria woke up to the smell of smoke. It was everywhere, cramming within the bedroom and stinging within her nostrils. The smell brought along a familiar panic that settled into her chest as if it had never left.She must have had an episode while sleeping and started a fire.Her eyes shot open to a terrifying black and had she not felt the toxins licking her skin she would have wondered if she'd gone blind.She screamed as she shot out of bed, tumbling to the floor and catching herself on palms flailing helplessly before her. Her eyes went ahead, saw the amber glowing in the slit between the bedroom door and its threshold. There had to be a minor inferno in the rest of the cabin to emit such smoke and she knew that she was supposed to be affected by the toxic whirls - for the first time, she thanked God she wasn't.Getting to the door wasn't particularly challenging even though she was virtually blind but as she gripped the handle she realized the metal was searing. Despite knowing she wasn't supposed to, Maria held on, felt the painful ecstacy rush to her head. For a second it settled her deathly anxiety and she tore the door open.

Charles had been reaching for the handle just as Maria came tumbling out the door. She held on to the frame, her wide eyes meeting his bloodshot ones. At first she didn't recognize him since the lower part of his face was covered by some kind of fabric and his body was stained by soot and sweat.The cabin was being eaten alive. Flames had gotten ahold of supportive beams as well as curtains, creating a sea of thrashing fire behind Charles. Somehow he'd managed to get to her room through it all and Maria felt heavy, sticky self-hatred reach for her alongside the flames as Charles grabbed a hold of her wrist and guided her through the cabin. He dodged the worst danger as he tried to get to the front door but the cabin was small and the fire particularly vicious."Watch out!" Maria yelled and pulled him backward just in time as a significant part of one of the beams upholding the ceiling came crashing down. They took cover the best they could as the charred wood spewed cinder and heat. It was almost staged, the way it landed just before the doorframe. The outside air blew onto it and further fueled the flames.Charles cursed but readied himself, cracking his knuckles and taking a deep breath despite the smoke. He reached for the beam."No!"Maria stopped him once again. She pulled him beside her and took his place, letting her hands hover above the glowing wood as she readied herself. She felt Charles try to stop her but he was too weak and, as much as she hated herself for it, the cabin fire only made her stronger.Her heart jolted as she placed her palms on the wood. Heat flushed her system, made her blood boil and breath steam as she exhaled violently from the shock. She was a living boiler pot. The pain was indescribable but the pure strength entwined with it was addicting.It could have been seconds or minutes before she let go, leaving the beam a charred skeleton, cool to the touch.

Maria fell out into the night. She briefly felt something she guessed as grass but her arms soon buckled under her, making her hit the ground straight on. Her body heaved and spasmed as smoke emitted from her pores. Fresh air replaced its dark cousin in her system but her lungs hated it, hastily pushing it back out.She was suffocating.Somehow she managed to tumble onto her back and Maria saw the sky above, disturbed by bulbous smoke rising up from the cabin. And she hated herself. She couldn't even mourn as she feared she was dying."Well would you look at that?"Maria's eyes shot open, a different kind of panic setting in. She tried to get her legs to do their job. Her body wouldn't listen to her and soon Buck's maleficent face replaced the sky."I knew you were here, but gambled a little when setting the fire.""Charles," she got out in the midst of her greedy breaths, barely lingering on the fact that she wasn't the reason for the fire. Her eyes flickered to what ever she could find."He's not here, must still be caught inside. Now come on, get up, that act won't work with me."Someone pulled Maria up by her upper arms, indelicately keeping her upright as her knees gave out. She threw her head back, drew a few deep breaths interrupted by her stomach contracting painfully.She looked back to the barrel of a sawed off shotgun between her eyes."I'm afraid this is the end for you, Maria."But it wasn't.Not two seconds later the shotgun was gone along with Buck. Then Neal was gone. He must have been judging by the way Maria fell to the ground. Her arms ached but she managed to get to her knees. She looked around the meadow. It was uncomfortably silent save for her own erratic breathing and the wood's crackling.

Someone kneeled before her and she almost cried with relief."Are you okay?" Charles asked, skimming her body for wounds."Neal and B-Buck... they just disappeared, I don't know what happened - I swear it wasn't me."He nodded slowly, looked around but didn't seem too concerned by her words. He grabbed her arm and hauled her up beside him."We need to get away.""The truck," Maria said, so relieved they were both alive that she felt her muscles relax slightly, only plagued by a dull ache instead of the slicing pain of a few seconds ago. She nodded to the red pickup only a few dozen metres away. "B-But maybe they'll come for us then.""T hey won't.""How do you know?""Because I killed them."Maria quieted. Through her hazy mind she recognized that she should be alarmed, but then again she wasn't completely harmless herself. "How could you kill them both?" They'd made it to the truck. Charles opened the passenger side, the old metal wailed loudly as if knowing he wasn't the owner, and maneuvered her into the seat. He remained standing beside her, giving her an indecipherable look. "I assure you," he said, "that we will both answer for questions. Later. Now we have to go." Maria couldn't have agreed more.

A/nOfficially a part of the Wattys! Please, please let me know if you like it, it helps a lot.

Chapter Six

S carreD

The car had been running for a while. It quaked and trembled with each minor rock rolling in underneath its wheels; on the seemingly random path Charles had chosen there were a lot. Maria felt a little sick but kept quiet. She didn't mention the branches scratching the windows, nor the bushes folding beneath the license plate. Charles supposedly stayed on track to Vinnar, despite the entire forest seeming to tell him there wasn't one.Maria sat still, threw the occasional glance his way but didn't conjur much of a reaction. Her body was drained from the prior onslaught of pain but she didn't feel like falling asleep after what had transpired in the past five hours."We're a sad pair," she said a little too loudly. The silence had become too unbearable. Charles was thrown out of what ever thoughts he'd been entertaining. His eyebrows furrowed."I'm completely fine," he responded with a shrug. "Maybe you feel sad.""You just killed two people, allegedly.""In self defense.""Still."He hummed. And that was that."Aren't you the least bit curious?" Maria insisted, turning to face him. He seemed to dislike that and focused on maneuvering around a particularly large birch."As I've told you, we both have things to answer for. But not her e.""Like how you got rid of Buck and Neal so fast... How did you even do that?""Later," he said, this time effectively ending the conversation."Stop the car."Charles gripped the wheel tighter, made an effort not to raise his voice. "I cannot.""I'm serious, stop the car now."He finally looked at her, expecting to see an angry face, but was met with a bundle of cloth and hair. She had curled up on the seat, hugging herself tightly. Her harsh breaths filled the car along with a faint yet definitive odor: smoke."What's happening?""Stop the car!"Charles indelicately pressed down on the brakes, making the car squeal for a moment until hitching and then stopping completely. By then Maria was nothing short of rolling out the door, landing on her side. A thousand knives burrowed into her cranium, each one hurting a different way. She hurriedly waved away Charles' reaching hands as he'd rounded the car.Maria somehow managed to get a few meters away from the truck using the surrounding trees as support before she fell into a heap on the forest floor, this time too hurt to get up."Stay away," she hissed, her voice much shriller than prior."What are you doing?""I know you didn't want to know about me yet," her body jumped, "but you might have to."Then her skin lit up.Charles took a few unstable steps backwards and watched, horrified, as Maria's body pulsated with light. It was just beneath her skin, surging past in a violent pace as if it was the blood itself that had begun glowing. She was screaming. Her hair was too weak to be able to contain the heat and it escaped in the form of flames, licking each strand.And then it was over. As quickly as it had come, the heat went. Maria was left sobbing in the middle of an imperfect circle of burnt moss. On her naked skin Charles noticed scars, old enough to have healed but so deep the scarred tissue was still an angry pink. Other than that the fire hadn't left any visible marks."Maria...""Water," she croaked. "I saw two bottles in the car."He didn't waste any time following her orders, still shaken. Whilst digging for the bottles he found an old coat. It smelled disgusting, but the chewy leather would cover her properly. He hurried to her, kneeled by her back and reached forward one of the bottles.She shook her head, winced, and then glanced back at him. Her eyes were red and swollen."Pour it.""But--""Please.""Maria." He reached for her shoulder but then pulled back just as quick. He looked at his palm. Blisters had begun forming.

Charles slowly stood back up. He undid the lid and tipped the bottle. The first water to hit her skin instantly dissipated, rose back up in the form of mist, but the second bottle seemed to work better. Maria stretched out her limbs as the water ran down her skin and once it'd been emptied, she began getting to her feet.Charles put the coat on her shoulders and she gripped it tightly on her way back to the car, not even looking at him."Are you sure you should get in?""It should be okay. The next episode won't be for at least another twelve hours."Charles helped her get in her seat. Then he looked back at the circle of dead moss."I don't know.""What?" he asked, looking back to her."What I am. I don't know, alright? You were going to ask, I could tell.""How long have you been doing... that?"Maria sniveled, cleared her throat and murmured, "Since forever. This might be a lot to take in but there are some things in this world you don't know about - supernatural things. And I'm one of them."Charles quieted for a second. He watched her slumping shoulders and felt the self-hatred come off her in overthrowing waves. For better or worse, he reached forward a hand."What are you doing?""Just watch."Under their gazes the hand transformed. The skin sprouted thick, black hair whilst the nails grew at such an impossible rate the cuticles cracked in the attempts to restrain them. Charles let out a brief groan as the bones cracked and repositioned, making the hand crooked and sharp. Beastly.Maria stared."There are two souls within me. One is human and the other much more... animalistic." He allowed his hand to return to its former, less disturbing state. "Supernatural enough for you?""I don't understand.""Some things aren't to be understood. They just are. Like me - and you, I'm guessing."Maria didn't say anything for a while. Then she lowered her head."Is it hereditary?" Charles asked, careful not to overstep boundaries which positions he had been much more certain of a few hours ago."I don't know.""What do you know?""Cages." Her eyes darkened considerably. "You might be fine with not understanding but my village.. they were obsessed. Thought I was a demon since birth but never really learnt anything more than the fact that I destroy things. They didn't want to. Imagine this little lighting show in the middle of squares and city halls for all to see." She spat on the ground. "No, cages is all I've ever known."Charles didn't respond."My scars, you must have seen them," she continued. Her voice was a tamed mixture of broken glass and shame."Not if you don't want me to.""I don't.""Then I didn't."She leant her head against the seat. Closed her eyes."Can we go now?"

A/nA little more insight this chapter, huh?Let me know if you like it!

Til next time

Chapter Seven

R attleD

Getting to Vinnar wasn't the relief that Maria had imagined it would be. If anything, the old shops and run-down playgrounds only made the hair on the back of her neck rise, sharing some agitated yet relatively harmless sparks between them. The truck entered the village with a cough and a moan before warily continuing on the desolate streets. It would occasionally stop completely, to have Charles rev it up again, but it didn't seem to matter much; there was not a single other vehicle being operated. "So this is Vinnar," Maria trailed. "It's off the radar. That's a good thing." "I know, but I don't see a single person here." Charles stopped the car, not bothering to get out of the street, and exited. He left the key in the ignition and the AC running. Maria frowned as she quickly undid her seatbelt and followed him out onto the street. She joined him by the hood of the car, a little rattled, asking, "What are you doing?" "This is where we part ways." "Really?" He nodded. Once. "You take the car and I'll find my way back." "To the cabin? It burned down." "No, I have a pack to tend to now that I failed my journey." His nonchalant expression was strained. "And you have a car to take to the other side of the world." Maria let her eyes wander from the brittle buildings and to the truck. She furrowed her brows."So there are more like you. Does that mean there are others like me, as well?""I don't know. But now is not the time to ponder. You need to leave."She nodded. Paused. Gave him a particular look."You're a good man, Charles. Even if you failed the journey."Charles nodded again before taking a few steps back towards where they'd emerged. He let his eyes scan Vinnar one last time before meeting the gaze of Maria still standing in the street."Good luck," he said. "What ever that entails.""You too."

Maria kept a firm grip on the steering wheel as another hail of pinecones came tumbling down from somewhere above. They assaulted the truck's windshield before rolling off, some getting stuck in the wipers while others damaging the paint. She sighed but thought it best to tear through the overgrown section of the woods - something she'd done more times than she could count in the lapsing hours - as quick as possible.Her foot went down on the gas, drawing a shrill cry from the vehicle before it jumped and charged forward. She made it back onto some kind of trail and decided to trust her instincts as she did a harsh left turn.The road was bumpy but she had to say that since exiting Vinnar and continuing through the forested areas, her surroundings were becoming more and more civil; a few hiking trails here, some chopped trees there. It all lead Maria to believe she was nearing another village - maybe this one with a trainstation.Something went against the truck.Maria lost balance at the same time the vehicle did. Her head hit the window, envoking a slight pain, and she managed to fall back into her seat just as the truck's right-side wheels hit the ground again. The engine was beyond salvation though, this time shutting off completely. Maria's eyes widened at the smoke seeping out from under the hood and the smell of petrol filling the car.Not thinking much about what had caused the malfunction, she hurried out of the seat and towards the hood. Opening it was a struggle but as she did, smoke spewed out of the machinery and blinded her.

At the same time the smoke somewhat dissipated, Maria knew she wasn't alone anymore. Something had made the car wheeze and sputter once more whilst she'd been distracted. She kept her gaze on the engine space and discreetly put her hand against one of the many hot metal components. The heat went directly to her ears and she could finally differentiate another set of sounds intertwined with the metal's creaking and engine's sighing: breaths.Maria rose her gaze at the same time the creature on the truck's roof let out a horrifying howl. She stumbled back, shocked, as the entire vehicle quaked under the animal's slightest movement. Was it an animal? It was hard to tell. Maria imagined it could be some kind of wolf but its size was off-throwing. Furthermore, the creature's back was arched in such a way it seemed capable of standing on its hind legs should it want to. Despite the fur there was something chillingly human about it.The creature pounced and, not seeming too strained, landed just inches before Maria. Its giant jaws shot open to reveal a dripping maw, ready to consume her. One of the deadly paws took a swipe, missing due to nothing more than chance. Maria's head recoiled and the act made her lose her balance.Despite her efforts at pulling herself back the beast was nearing with clear intentions. Each step was purposeful, dead eyes watching her fear increase with every failed attempt she made at getting away.Maria watched the claws, imagined what it would be like to have them burrow into her cranium. Even in the havoc she couldn't help looking at them. They were incredibly disturbing yet strangely familiar.Where had she seen them before?She made a wrong move and twisted her wrist painfully. She fell back. The beast took the oppurtunity to pounce. Its sharp maw was soon above her face, closing in at a dangerous pace. Hot, ransid air blew into her mouth.That was all she needed.Not stopping to ponder, Maria placed her hands on the sides of the animal's face and allowed the chest to open. All at once, incredible heat surged to her fingers.The beast flew off the ground seconds before Maria did the same. She looked around but couldn't find it anymore. Instead she found herself surrounded by ten others. The same yet different. Each one looked just as bloodthirsty as their companion.Maria raised her hands, earning a chorus of chilling growls, and tried to get as far away from any nipping mouths as possible. This left her in the middle of a continously shrinking circle.Her eyes went to their trampling paws.Then they widened."Charles! Is he here?"Nobody answered but the animals definitely reacted, some stopping and some nervously throwing their massive heads about."I think I know one of you. Charles," she repeated. She looked around, desperately searching for any sort of intelligence hiding within the black eyes. "He's your leader, isn't he?"A little more commotion."He's a friend of mine, I swear, I swear!""Can you prove that?"The voice, if somewhat burly, was a relief to hear.The one who'd spoken was behind her. He stood amongst the beasts, naked and dirty but definitely a human. His eyes were narrowed, his posture everything but warm.Maria gulped."Get him. He'll confirm everything. ""You just hurt one of his packmates... I don't think you want him to find you.""Your packmate just tried to kill his friend. Maybe I'm not the only one in danger."Silence."Keep an eye on her. I will get him. She makes a move, kill her... Let's see if you're as close as you say you are."

A/nLeaving Turkey tonight :(

Chapter Eight

D^{eN}

The animals Maria had been left with weren't in any sense of the word tame. She knew this because, despite the instruction to simply watch her, she was continously fighting off nipping teeth and swiping paws. Occasionally one would leap across the circle, forcing her to jump back. It was all fear tactics, she knew that very well but was starting to get a little pissed off. She had to aim her palms against the ground just to make sure she wouldn't accidentally harm yet another one of the beasts.Charles watched it all play out.Kripin stood next to him, both a little ways outside the crowd and both with their arms crossed, a grim expression playing on their faces. Nobody had noticed them yet."So she's actually telling the truth... You are friends.""I wouldn't go that far," Charles responded, watching the exhasparated Maria cuss out one of the packmembers that had tried to take a bite out of the leather coat."She did."He hummed disapprovingly before settling on, "She's a good person.""Well, she hurt one of the youths pretty badly so I have to ask." Kripin glanced up at his leader. "Is she good enough to be spared?""She saved my life."Kripin remained silent but nodded. Once."I'll fix this," Charles said before making his way towards the crowd, allowing his scent to fill the vicinity.The pack grew wilder, bumped against eachother and yipped and howled. Maria grew scared before she saw Charles enter the circle. The animals gave him some room but he didn't stop until he stood a metre or two from her. He crossed his arms. Maria flinched as one particularly loud animal let out a feral growl.Charles raised his hand.The pack quieted."Thank you," Maria said, exhasperated, while pulling on the coat."Why are you here?"She pointed to the truck but Charles only spared it a brief flicker of interest."One of your friends went against it.""You ran one over?""No!" Maria pointed to the truck again, this time at the dent on the passenger-side door. "It went against it. See? Must have thought I was food. But then I explained that we knew eachother and, err, could you please tell them we know eachother?"Charles gave her a long look before calling over his shoulder, "We know eachother."The animals instantly dispersed. Some went back into the trees, some made a point of running past Maria, almost making her tumble to the ground from the sheer force. Once they'd all cleared out Charles and Maria remained.Maria looked to the spot where the last creature had dissappeared."So you are their leader of sorts?""I am an alpha, yes. But that doesn't matter now, it's starting to rain."She looked up to the clear skies, listened to the birds chirping."It's not raining.""It will," he insisted as if it was the most obvious thing in the world. "Make sure you get to another town soon.""I can't, the engine is fried."Charles stood silent for an abundance of seconds before nodding, turning around, and beginning to walk in the direction most of the creatures had gone. As he was almost out of sight, he glanced at her over his shoulder and jerked his chin in a message she understood clearly: come here.

"Where are we going?" Maria asked once she'd joined up with Charles. He didn't answer right away but it wasn't because he was rude; some trees seemed to be very interesting. He let his finger run down a few fresh scratches in the bark and then brought them to his nose before humming thoughtfully and continuing."I'm bringing you to my den.""Really?""Until I figure out a way to get you to where you need to go."Maria almost stumbled on a root but managed to keep upright."Listen, I really appreciate that, but I don't think I'm made for living in a hole in the ground."Charles stopped to smell another tree, this one leaving a frown on his face."These woods aren't safe. You're lucky the worst to find you was my pack.""Didn't feel very lucky," Maria grumbled but he didn't seem to hear her.Charles stopped as suddenly as the trees did. He stepped aside, allowing Maria to enter the large clearing, and let her take it all in."Holy shit."The clearing was bustling with life, an oasis in the middle of the deserted forest. There were people everywhere - but even more beasts - and each one was heaving, planting, or destroying something. A few cubs were fighting under the watchful eye of a man stringing up fabric whilst, a little ways down, two young men in armor were being lectured by a burly woman on how to properly swing a sword. The clearing wasn't leveled, meaning the left hand side rose into a hill. Lining the lower tree line were quaint cabins. A large wooden house sat perched on top the highest point, overlooking the area."I-I don't know what to say."Charles shrugged but couldn't hide how proud he was of his people. A few bowed as they saw him and he nodded in recognition, but he didn't want to stand around any longer."Come on.""What?""I told you, I'm taking you to my den."Maria nodded, still not completely finished with the view but nevertheless began to move towards the cabins.A hand landed on her shoulder, spun her around. Charles' furrowed brows met her."What are you doing?" he asked."I thought we were going to your den."He looked from her to the cabins and then back again before shaking his head. His finger flew out, pointed up the hill, to the large house."That's my den."

A/nAnother one lmao

Chapter Nine

E lementS

It was raining. Hard. The clearing was empty, the cabins' windows glowing yellow as every inhabitant had gone inside to take cover. Left were fabric and weapons and stray flowers putting up a tough fight against the rough downpour. Somewhere far off thunder crackled but it wasn't near enough to cause any more disturbance than a vague vibrato. Maria watched it all with her legs folded underneath her and her hair glued to her head. She sat on top the hill, just before Charles' den, and shuddered under the elements. Goosebumps rose like splattered paint on the skin exposed from underneath the coat. She could have worn something warmer, like the clothes she'd been offered inside, and spent her evening in the bed Charles had been nice enough to give her. But she didn't think it wise. A mental count down had begun: it was soon time for another episode. When it came she didn't want to ruin more than she already had. "It's raining." Charles took place behind her, cocked his head when watching her sorry frame. He was warm, the glow of the lanterns from inside the den almost glued to him, but the aggressive droplets had already begun making him one with the dark scenery. "It is," Maria hummed, eyeing a bug scurrying past her hand. "Why are you out here?" "It's almost time."

Charles opened his mouth but then closed it again. He watched the view himself."You look cold.""I am cold," Maria answered in the same bland tone but couldn't hide from him how scared she was of the pain that she knew would come. "It's by choice, though. I'm savoring it while I can."A cloud of mist rose from Maria in a split second. As it dissipated, her hair was dry and her face flushed. The rain soon drenched her again, though, making her shrink."See?""You seem to have pretty good control of it," Charles commented.Maria nodded, adding, "It's just the episodes... They're impossible to hold back."Maria let out a scream as two hands grabbed her and hauled her up to her feet. She was spun to finally look at Charles. He had an indecipherable expression."What are you doing?""I want to try something. Close your eyes.""Charles, it's almost time--""Trust me."For some reason she did."Now, imagine your powers as an orb.""It's a chest," she interjected."A chest... Alright. I want you to close this chest, and trap everything within it. Everything. When you feel the episode coming on, I want you to push down the chest. I want you to push, and push, and not stop until it's in your feet. Press it through bone and skin and muscle - do what you have to do.""I don't know if it's going to work.""Try it."Maria let her eyes flutter open and was for some reason surprised to see Charles still holding her. She gave him a look she wasn't certain was wise."Alright," she murmured. "Once it comes, I will. Where have you learnt this?""Each full moon is a hard time for my kind. Many lose control if not taught how to suppress their urges.""Your kind..." Maria trailed, looking down in a poor attempt to hide her envy. "You have all these people to support you. I have no one."Surprisingly warm fingers found her chin. The warmth was different from the melted metal running through her veins, different from the fire's heated ache. She looked up and briefly wondered why she'd never noticed how beautiful his eyes were. Especially when as transfixed to her as they were currently.She got closer, lowered her gaze to rest on something even more alluring: his lips.Charles' left hand hooked the back of her neck, tolerating the excited sparks hopping off her hair and nipping at his fingers. He lowered his head. Perhaps it was the heat of her skin in the cold air, perhaps it was her loneliness, begging to be held, but in that second he wanted her. God, he wanted her so much it hurt.A few more centimeters, and he would have her. Just a few.Maria pushed him away.

Charles stumbled back, more than a little surprised, and didn't even have time to dodge the coat flying at his face a moment later. He frowned, pulled the leather off his head, and saw Maria a few meters away, hunched over."It's happening," she gritted out.Charles threw the coat aside and closed the distance, grabbing her arm as to make her stand up straight. Her skin was hot, but not yet searing."No!" she hissed. "Step away, you'll get killed.""The chest, Maria. Close it and push it down. Now.""Please, please don't touch me."Charles made sure he caught her gaze and then assured, "I trust you. Now push it down, before it goes too far."She hesitated, seemed to deliberate whether to just try and get him off, but then closed her eyes. Her erratic breathing didn't slow but it was obvious she was trying to control it. Within her, she pictured the chest. As Charles had told her, Maria put it all in there. The powers, the emotions, and, just to be safe, the feeling of Charles' hands holding her upright.She began forcing it down. It was painful but not comparable to catching fire so she continued. It got stuck, tried to open up sometimes, but she somehow managed to force it down to her feet."Charles?" Maria whispered, not daring to open her eyes in the possibility she would see a charred skeleton.The hand on her arm squeezed. Once. It was the confirmation she needed to dare to open her eyes."You did it."Maria could cry. She let go of his arm, noted how the most damage she'd left behind was the trace of her nails, and wiggled her fingers. No pain."I can't believe it."Maria was in awe. She began moving her legs but the action was too sudden and left her a wobbly mess hanging around Charles' neck. Not that it mattered."Look," Charles said, pointing somewhere behind her.She looked over her shoulder, the act making her dizzy, and saw what he'd been reffering to. In the spot where she'd just stood were two burning footprints quickly being doused by the rain."Maybe I need a little more practise."Charles threw the coat over her shoulders."I'm taking you inside.""Wait."Maria narrowed her eyes. Something had caught her attention, something moving in the treeline ahead of them."Do you see that?" she asked. "I think they're... people."Charles moved in front of her, looked to where she'd pointed, and let out a disdained grunt. He sniffed the air."Humans and... gunpowder. We have to get inside."

A/nCliffhanger and romantic scene in one chapter? Christmas came early.

Can I ask a question? There will be some sex in this story and I wonder what's best, leaving "the act" itself unspoken or writing it out. What do you want? Please let me know what you prefer when reading a story.

xoxo

Chapter Ten

L ynN

Maria counted her fingers, watched the fire dance between them as if nothing had happened. Charles sat by the kitchen window, watching the outdoors. He'd been there since they made it inside and insisted that Maria remained in one of the large armchairs in the livingroom. She had soon dragged it into the kitchen, watching Charles watching the outdoors.

"You can just say it, you know."Charles jumped and whipped his head around. He gave her a look as if he hadn't noticed she was in there with him."Say what?""You think it's them, the people from my village.""It's a possibility.""It's more than a possibility. I know it's them, I recognized one. Lynn, the leader of the civilian troop."Charles frowned."They're a group of five or six that are responsible of keeping the village safe. It doesn't matter. Look, I know what's happening here."He wasn't looking at her anymore. If he had then he'd undoubtedly see the moisture she was blinking into her lashes."You do?""Yes. These people are a threat to your pack and we both know it and right now you're trying to figure out a way to tell me to leave."That caught his attention."You've been more than kind," Maria continued, getting up from the chair. "And I don't want to make this hard on you so I'll do you a favor since you've done me so many already, and just leave.""Maria--""No, no, it's fine. There are kids here and elderly - I saw them - and if Lynn finds out what you are then... No, It's better that I take my chances out there."A hand reached for her but she swatted it off. Another then came, grabbing her upper arm."You are not going out there," Charles said, his expression a product of harsh lines and anger. She couldn't tell if it was directed at her or not. "My pack is well protected. You, however, are not.""You don't know Lynn.""I don't, but I do know they've left the property a long time ago.""How do you..."Charles put a finger to his nose and, once certain Maria wouldn't try to run off, let go of her arm. He took a careful step back."You know they will come back, right? They must have seen me and then you and reckoned they needed more people.""Of course. But by then we'll have a plan.""You will?"He shook his head."We will. You have insight. Like it or not but you're an asset now. These people are threats to my pack and you're going to help me eliminate them. I can't let you go."Maria knew he was just saying what she wanted to hear but nevertheless sunk back into the armchair with a relief so strong when surging through her body that it made her knees weak.She didn't notice how relieved her decision had made Charles. "Thank you," she whispered sincerely. "I don't even know what to say.""Tell me about your village.""There's... not much to tell. They don't care about much. It's a small community, no more than two hundred people, crammed into a wooded area just south of your cabin - sorry about that by the way.""It wasn't mine," he reassured.She thought for a second."Before I came along I don't think they were very well versed with anything... not human. I still don't think they are, but now they're obsessed with wanting to be. The mayor, John Gooden, let's it all slide because he wants to be re-elected. God, the only thing he cares about is being able to go to that pompous ball.""A ball. Do you mean the annual one? What's it called..."Maria nodded, tried to remember what she'd heard Lynn and the others talk about outside her cell."The one at Hillbury Manor to honor all the small communities in the Hillbury county, yeah. He goes there every year. Religiously."Charles had pulled out a chair some time during their conversation and was now sitting right in front of her, elbows on his thighs and eyes somewhere far off."When is that?""I'm afraid I don't know.""You've never gone?" Charles asked before he could think to stop himself.She shrunk back into the chair a little. "I'll ask someone," he quickly continued. "But I think it's nearing.""What does it matter?"Charles shook his head and stood up, motioning for her to follow before exiting the kitchen.

They made it to the room where Maria had previously been told she would stay. She walked inside, plopped down on the bed, and frowned. She threw a look to Charles who was still in the doorframe, arms crossed and face as indecipherable as usual."You need to sleep," he stated."But Lynn and the others, and the plan--""Sleep. For as long as you'd like. We'll get started tomorrow.""I won't be able to sleep," she murmured.

Charles left, going back into the kitchen. He was just about to sit down by the window when something caught his eye: the clothes he'd brought out for her, thrown on top the back of a chair. He thought to the burly coat and how uncomfortable it had to be.Within a few seconds he was back at the opening to her bedroom, raising his hand to knock on the frame but stopping himself as he saw Maria. She was already underneath the covers, the sheet pulled up to her chin. Covering the pillows was her unruly hair, stained with soot and damp from the rain. Her eyes were closed, her breathing heavy. On the floor was the discarded leather coat.

A/nHope you like it! Maybe a lil boring but I think you get a little more insight into everything. Til next time!

Chapter Eleven

T he plaN

Maria stared at Kripin. He stared back. She crossed her arms, leant against the frame. He sunk further into the couch. Maria instantly regretted entering the livingroom at all - was it too late to go back to bed?"Where's Charles?" she asked, clearing her throat from sleep."He'll be in shortly.""And why are you here?""I could ask the same thing."Maria knew how she must look but fought the urge to comb through her hair and pull on the coat, not wanting him to have the satisfaction."He will make a full recovery," Kripin broke through the silence, his voice so sharp it made Maria jump. "The packmember you injured.""Oh, thank God.""Oh, that's... unfortunate."Kripin's face darkened. He eyed her with a certain look she'd seen a hundred times before, trying to determine if she was a threat or not. It didn't really bother her. What ever his conclusion was, he didn't have time to act on it as they both heard the door slam closed from across the den.

Charles entered the livingroom and threw down a duffel bag onto the floor. He bent down, began digging through it, but then froze. His nose scrunched. He looked to Maria."Good morning," she murmured."It's the middle of the day.""I trust you slept well," Charles said, ignoring Kripin's remarks. Maria decided to do the same. She took a few steps towards the bag, noticed the scratches and patches of dirt."I've been doing some work. ""Clearly. This looks a little beat up, are you okay?"Kripin released a sound and stood up. He pulled out the bag from under Maria's nose, earning a nasty glare, and went into the kitchen. As they'd all made it, Kripin placed the duffel bag on the table and crossed his arms."Does she know anything, boss?" Charles shook his head."Know what?" Maria interjected, taking a seat near the bag. Kripin noticed and gave a disdained grimace but didn't say anything. Both of them looked to Charles."We are going to infiltrate the Hillbury Ball."

Maria was at once very happy that she was sitting down. Her hands were suddenly over her mouth but then she couldn't breathe and she instead put them down on the table. Her fingerprints branded into the wood."No," she said slowly. "You can't do that, why would you do that?""We're going to find mayor Gooden.""And do what?" She quickly retracted her hands. "Oh no, are you going to kill him?""Of course not," Kripin snapped. "But he doesn't know that. The plan is to talk to him, convince him to keep his 'civilian troop' away.""You mean you're going to threaten him."The two men shared a look."I've been gathering a few things this morning. Tickets, IDs, proper clothes from higher ups. It wasn't perfect given the time frame but we won't be found out. The ball is the first saturday of every august," Charles informed, avoiding her pressing gaze. "We imagine we can get in and out before raising alarm.""You do, do you?" Maria questioned with a pointed look directed at Kripin. Then she noticed the smell of burnt wood and quickly retracted her hands from the table."You're coming, too, pyro."Maria's head whipped to Charles. He looked disapproving of Kripin's harsh words but didn't argue against him."No," she repeated. "I won't be able to help anyway. No. I can't meet him again. I will not.""You won't," Charles said, successfully intercepting Kripin. "We need you to identify him, that is all.""This is crazy.""It's necessary.""Charles--""This is bigger than you, Maria, and you won't come to any harm."Maria shot up from her chair, slamming a palm down on the table. She opened her mouth. Then closed it. Her angry expression fell flat at the same time her gaze met Charles'. It was replaced by one much less enjoyable."You can't promise that."And then she exited the kitchen.

An hour passed before Charles found Maria. She had then returned to her room and, as Charles entered, finished putting on the set of clothes she'd been offered. They were pale and stiff, nothing like her, but would grant more protection against the weather than the coat.She saw him enter through the mirror and did the last button. She smiled wearily. "I'm sorry for how I reacted back there.""Your safety would be prioritized, Maria.""I'll do it.""Oh, you are?"She nodded and observed herself in the mirror, running her palms down the skirt."I look very normal, don't I?""Like you're one of us."Maria tried not to show how much that hurt. She turned around, eyes steely again. She motioned towards the bed.Charles sat down."I'll just be going in and out, right?""Yes. We'll have a few other packmembers along and once you give the signal, we engage and you make your exit.""Sounds easy enough... but, err, Charles?"He frowned, eyeing her fiddling hands, and nodded, not actually certain he wanted to hear what it was she was going to say."I'll come along, but I need a guarantee. From you.""Anything.""I've been trying to escape from these people for my entire life, and we are now about to willingly enter a nest full of them. There is a chance they'll recognize me. And there is a chance they'll want to take me back.""They won't. But if they do then I'll break you out. You have my word."Maria shook her head and seemed to grow even more anxious."I escaped once. It was hard, and I barely even made it - I know I won't be getting out again. So, if they get me then I need you to..."Charles didn't understand. He refused to. Maria saw the struggle in his eyes and sat down beside him. She took his hand. Guided it to her throat."If they take me I need you to make sure I don't go back there. By any means necessary."Cha rles quickly pulled back his hand, watched her with a horrified face."What did they do to you?""Enough for me to know that I can't stand even a second more of it."Maria repressed the anxious heat but it still glowed faintly underneath her skin."Promise me," she murmured."You can't ask that.""Please. Promise me this and I'll help however I can."Silence. The longest silence in the history of the universe."Alright... I promise. If you get caught," Charles' right hand transformed into its more beastly state, "then I'll kill you."

A/n

Woop de do, here it is

Chapter Twelve

C hapter Twelve

Maria dodged a fatal blow. Her eyes caught the slight movement in her peripheral as some hairs fell to the ground, victim to the blade. She dove to the mat, rolled to the left as a boot clamped down just right of her head. Another aimed for her exposed wrist but she managed to get away there too.Maria pulled her knees underneath her and, after blindly sending out a surge of fire, staggered to her feet. She threw her hair back.The fire had caught Kripin slightly off-guard but he was quickly preparing for another attack. He gripped the dagger tighter, his calculating eyes shooting around her body. They lingered on her glowing hands. He seemed to consider attacking once more but then paused and straightened. He threw the dagger to the ground, stretched his fingers and let his eyes narrow at her briefly in a silent threat before smiling.The circle of younger packmembers surrounding them laughed warily."And that is how you use the dagger even when your opponent has otherwordly abilities," Kripin said. "Don't let its size fool you, there will be times when it's all you have at your disposal. Wouldn't you say its quite effective, Maria?"She shot him a glare."Nevermind. Today's lesson is over. Tomorrow you will be the ones practicing your handling so make sure you've found a partner by then."

It wasn't until every youngster had vacated the small cottage that Maria felt it safe to take her eyes off Kripin. Even then it was just to step off the mat."I don't see why you had to use me.""You've been burrowing in Alpha's den for a few days. Now it seems you're staying here indefinitely, and I thought it best you make yourself useful."He didn't feel completely comfortable turning his back on her either but nevertheless began rolling up the mat." Still. You could have told me what we were doing," she growled, rolling her shoulder still aching from his first, rather unanticipated, punch. "I could have hurt you.""I doubt it.""I hurt your friend, didn't I?"He was by her feet at that point. He paused his rolling and scowled up at her."Listen, pyro, don't think for a second that I'm afraid of you.""Then don't expect me to be fine with you pushing me around," she spat back. "I'm not a part of your pack, dog. I don't need your blessing."Kripin shot to his feet. His face was centimeters from her."What did you call me?" he hissed."Careful," Maria smirked, feeling power tingle in her fingertips. "You're running pretty hot."He took in her words. Paused. Then took an adamant step back. Just as he grabbed the mat off the floor, the door flew open between them. Both jumped.Charles' dark gaze flew over the small space, immediately finding a flushed Maria and tense Kripin growing the distance between them."Hi, boss.""I heard there was a fight.""Just practice. Harmless," Kripin assured, earning a sharp look from Maria.Charles nodded towards the far-end wall. They all turned to see a smoking burn mark, burrowing well into the wood."That doesn't look very harmless."Maria and Kripin both refused to meet his gaze."Two weeks. That's it. You think you can manage without killing each other?""Yes, boss - sorry, boss.""Sorry, Charles."A subtle glare from Kripin that Charles thankfully either didn't notice or chose to ign ore."Good. Maria, you're coming with me to the den. Kripin... clean this up immediately."An adamant silence."Yessir."

"Forgive me, Charles, I didn't mean to start any trouble," Maria said once the door had slammed shut to the alpha's den. It was the first sentence either one had uttered in the walk between the training facilities and

Charles' house. She looked down at her hands, followed him into the kitc hen."You shouldn't have allowed yourself to come in harm's way," Charles said, looking through cupboards instead of her."I didn't get hurt. Not too badly.""You're bleeding," he explained and pulled out a small wooden box from a drawer just above him.Maria looked down and, to her surprise, Charles had been right. The dagger must've gotten her in the midst of it all and a thin stream of blood was now trickling down her outer thigh."Si t."Without much fuss, Maria hopped up on the wooden counter. Charles positioned himself in front of her and opened the wooden box. Inside was a neat collection of cotton swabs, bandage wraps and a clear liquid bubbling within a small bottle. As if he'd done it a thousand times, Charles took a cotton swab and doused it in the clear liquid before putting the box aside.He brought up her skirt to reveal the wound."I really am sorry," Maria murmured as he pressed the soft material against the cut. "I didn't know we were going to cause such a ruckus.""Can I give you a word of warning?"She tried to ignore the sensation of his fingers riding up her skirt further and nodded."I don't fully know what we are," he continued. "But I do know we are predators. We're sly and dangerous, some more than others. You shouldn't have allowed yourself to be lured in."Maria drew a harsh breath as the liquid stung at a particularly deep part of the cut."You should never be alone with a predator," he ended, pulling back the cotton and instead taking out the bandage."But I'm alone with you.""Do not for a second mistake me for a common specimen, Maria. I'm one of the strongest of my kind, and yet I can still feel your blood from meters away, calling to me. You're strong, but don't underestimate a hungry carnivore."Maria sat silent, not sure what to respond, until he bit off a piece of bandage."What are you doing with that?" she asked."Stopping the bleeding.""No, it's not necessary.""Maria, I just told you, you can't go around bleeding here.""No," she interjected and brought her skirt back up to reveal the wound. "That's not what I meant."Under Charles' watchful gaze, Maria put her index finger to the cut. Her fingertip heated to the point of almost catching fire and she then pressed it against the severed skin. She ran it down the length of the cut, leaving skin melted shut behind. By the time she was done there was a clean, if not a bit wobbly, scar left behind. But no blood. Maria sweated as she let her skirt fall back and said, "See? Just as new." "How did you learn to do this?" Her gaze darkened but, as oppose to other times, she seemed to want to talk about her past. "I had to," she said lowly. "I realized that when I was around seven, after a particularly gruesome converting therapy session." "Converting therapy?" "You've seen the scars..." "And it all fell into place." "They tortured you. Just to try and remove your powers?" Maria neither confirmed nor denied. Instead she said, "I've been saved from bleeding out a lot of times using this method." "Maria, I don't--" "I'm going to go to bed. If that's alright with you." Not waiting for an answer, she hopped off the counter and gave a weak smile not reaching her eyes before staggering off. Charles watched after her until he heard the door to her room open and close. He then quickly turned around and headed for the hallway.

"Boss? What are you doing here?" Before Kripin could say anything else, he was thrown back, crashing into his hallway's wall before tumbling to the ground. He quickly got up, ready to fight back, when he saw Charles' livid face in his doorway. They knew very well he couldn't harm his Alpha. With wary eyes, he lowered his fists. "I don't want you to hurt Maria anymore, Kripin." "What? Boss--" "This isn't a request, Kripin. I do not wish to discuss it. Have I made myself clear?" There were a hundred things he wanted to say but forcedly repressed them. He lowered his head. "Yessir." "Good. Tomorrow I do not wish to be disturbed with any news similar to the ones I recieved today, and if I do then you'll be to blame." "Yessir." Charles nodded, seemed to want to do more, but then turned back around. He exited the cabin with a roaring heart and let the door slam behind him without another look Kripin's way. His gaze ascended to his den where Maria was probably asleep. She would remain unaware of what he'd done for her. He'd make sure of it.

Or it would just complicate things further.

A/nGoals, amirite?

Chapter Thirteen

Handmaid

Maria never awoke with the sun. She wasn't certain if it had something to do with her powers or if it was simply her unhealthy sleeping-habits which were to blame, but she rarely found it in her to wake up before the late rays had warmed the room to a buzzing temperature.The handmaid outside her door didn't have that rule.There she stood, rigid and stern at the break of dawn, unwavering under Maria's disdained gaze and unruly hair crackling with agitated sparks."I'm here to get you sorted."Maria's mind didn't link her thoughts to her mouth fast enough and so by the time she parted her lips, the handmaid had already entered the room and emitted several disgruntled huffs and puffs."Sorted?" Maria groaned, just the same as the door falling shut behind her."Yes. Sorted. You apparently have something important tomorrow and Alpha thought it best to get a head start.""I don't have anything tomorrow, as far as I know... Did he say what it was?"The chambermaid huffed another time and hurried back to the door, tearing it wide open with surprising force. In came a gaggle of young women, some holding brushes and others trying to keep silk fabrics from touching the floor as they entered. Maria widened her eyes. Last but not least was a team of four, heaving a wooden tub between them.

It was filled with steaming water splashing about, trying to jump over the edge, but surprisingly little had actually spilled once it was placed down in the middle of the room."He mentioned a ball."Maria paused her horrific staring at the tub to instead aim her wide eyes at the old woman."A ball -- the ball? That can't be right. What day is it?"Not bothering to wait for an answer, Maria began counting her fingers. The women watched. She landed on her index finally, lowering her hand with a blank stare."It's tomorrow..." she murmured.Maria felt stupid for forgetting but didn't find it incredible. She'd been holed up in the Den most of the first week and following the night when her and Kripkin got into a fight, she'd seen very little of both him and Charles. She hadn't been sure what she was allowed to do and had settled on staying in bed, catching up on long overdue rest.And now it had come back to bite her."Get in the tub, please."

Being sorted was a tedious task for both Maria and the women. In her now riled up state, she was running fairly hot - the tub had to be re-filled several times as the water evaporated. Once that was done and she'd been scrubbed, doused in lavender, and gotten her hair put into braids that were easier to handle than "the rat's nest on top her head", everyone was rather tired of eachother. Some girls sucked on the small burn-marks on their fingers while others mourned the loss of their favorite brush or sponge, a melted victim to the heat."So, what now?" Maria trailed, standing in the middle of the room, only a robe hanging off her shoulders."What else can we do?" an anonymous voice spat. "You're making this impossible.""Why is this ball even important? And why are you allowed to go?" another girl piped up.A parade of hums showed that many agreed. And then suddenly all eyes were on Maria. Caught off-guard and quite done with it all herself, she decided to be honest.To an extent."I'm not the one who wants this," she said, exhasparated. "It's Charles! It's all his fault."Murmurs erupted. Some commented on her speaking ill of their Alpha and some thought it strange she uttered his name at all."Are you and Alpha... friends?"Maria paused alongside the chatter. She tried to find the source of the voice but it was a hopeless cause. She supposed honesty was the only way now that she'd begun. And, God, was it refreshing."I don't know. I thought we were, that we had something special, but then he just...""Went off?"She nodded.A symphony of agreeing murmurs hugged her tightly, validated her frustration."They do that," a woman piped up. Her mouth was pulled together in a bitter expression. She was heavily pregnant. "Sometimes they just leave, even the good ones.""But why?""It's just the way it is, sweetie. You'll do best staying out of Alpha's line of sight, I reckon."Maria's head sunk further down between her shoulders. She felt awful. She just wanted to hop back into bed and, God be merciful, not wake up again.

A small hand was put to her shoulder, squeezed meekly. It was a teenage girl, no more than seventeen summers. She nodded as if she understood even though Maria wondered if that was possible.The next hand, this one landing on her other shoulder, belonged to a woman much older. Running down the length of her face was a nasty scar. She nodded as well."These males can be unpredictable," the pregnant woman piped up again. "Us females - especially the lower ranking ones - have to have each other's backs. You may not be a part of the pack but you're clearly important, other-wise Alpha wouldn't indulge you, so consider yourself having of allies, fire girl."It was then Maria realized that the warning she'd recieved from Charles about predatory instincts hadn't applied to her simply because she was an outsider, but it applied to packmembers as well. She looked around her. Some women were hugging as bad memories surfaced, some looked empowered by the pregnant woman's words.Maria let her hands be swallowed by flames."And if you ever need an edge," she said, looking to the faces around her illuminated by her hands, "consider yourselves in possession of fire itself."

A/nSorry it's been so long. Truly. But I'm in the middle of a big move and have just started a new school so it's pretty hard to squeeze in writing.

I'll hurry better with the next update.

Please let me know if you like it<3

Chapter Fourteen

H^{igH}

Maria stared out the window. The forest was dark, much too dark for her eyes to find any particular body to focus on. But they didn't need to. For the past hour she'd found something much more foreign to observe: herself. Her reflection was vague and a bit distorted, only illuminated by the light in the car's ceiling. Her eyes, accentuated and beautiful, were framed by the creasing of her worried brows. Just barely grazing her cheek was an orange lock of hair that had tore free from the confinement of the pins. Her lips were red. And dark. She'd been told they matched her dress (as did the nail polish she'd begun scraping off the second she got in the car). Maria couldn't help but feel like a phony, like she'd be stopped before she even entered. "You're nervous," Charles said, marking the end of a 30 minute-silence. He sat in the seat opposite her, hands on his thighs and a tie around his neck. He didn't give away a single thing. "Yeah," Maria said, putting her hands on her thighs as well. "It feels like my heart is beating out my chest.""That's impossible.""Aren't you going to tell me to calm down? Relax?""No. We are about to attempt to threaten a village head into following our orders. It's a highly dangerous operation, performed by just the three of us. You should be alarmed."Maria crossed her arms."Shouldn't

Kripin be here?"The small hatch left of Charles' head opened and Kripin's voice came flooding into the back: "Do you see anyone else wanting to drive, pyro? Maybe you want the whole pack to get involved.""I get why you don't want to risk the pack!" she bit back. "But I don't get why you won't come along inside with us.""He will," Charles said before closing the hatch. "But he will slink by unnoticed, keep an eye out. It's always good to have a card up your sleeve."

It wasn't long before the terrain changed. The elderly trees thinned and the paths became roads. A few cars appeared behind them, all heading in the same direction, while Maria tried her best to get a good look ahead.

The community surrounding Hillbury Manor was small and the people scarce. It was clear their entourage was one of the biggest happenings of the year; mothers stood in the doors of their modest homes, holding children pointing with wide eyes and slacked jaws as the cars rolled past. A few young men and women tried to chase after them, carrying baskets of fruits and pouches filled with coins. Their nakes toes sunk into the mudded road. It was clear they thought this a good oppurtunity to make a buck.Maria turned to Charles who was already looking at her with an odd frown."The Hillburys have ruled the county for ages, I thought they collected a small percentage of the taxes from its inhabitants?""They do.""Then shouldn't they be rich? These people are no better off than the ones from my own village."Charles shook his head, fixed his already impeccable collar."Make no mistake, the Hillbury family hold incredible wealth and influence, but there is a reason they made it this far. They have had to be ruthless. And selfish. The people of the Hillbury village have no larger share of their fortune than you and I."As if hearing them, one of the salesmen carrying baskets knocked on Maria's window. He nodded happily, keeping up with the vehicle, clearly wanting her to roll down her window.She was relieved as he went on."I don't know if I like the Hillburys much.""Good," Charles muttered, watching the salesman fall back. "It's a show of character."

Maria wasn't ready as the car door opened -- she was even less ready for the Hillbury Manor's overwhelming presence. Similar to Charles' den it overlooked the modest village but whilst Charles' home was warm and grounded, the manor was almost too much for Maria. Each pillar, each colored window, even the flowers planted outside, were the opposite of the community a little ways down.Maria's mouth soured with the suspicion that that had been the point.An arm snaked around hers, forced her to begin moving towards the giant doorway lined with suited men holding swords. Behind her more cars drove into the graveled courtyard and beautiful women and men all gravitated to the entrance like moths to a million-dollar flame."There are like eight thousand companies here.""Forty-three actually.""I'll stand out like a sore thumb."Maria's heel snagged on the uneven ground and Charles discreetly leant her his balance."This is good. The more people there are, the less chance you'll get recognized. Remember, you won't be here for long."The walk to the entrance felt like miles and once they made it inside, Maria's nerves only worsened. There were people everywhere, their luxurious selves filling the equally expensive ballroom. A drink was placed in her hand. She was about to give it back to the server when she noticed that most held on to one."See him?" Charles asked lowly, accepting a glass as well.Maria scanned the colorful dresses and suits, tried to shut out the cheerful trumpets."No. No, I don't think so.""Alright. Blend in. See if you can find him. I'll come to you soon enough."Maria watched in horror as he reclaimed his arm."You're not coming with me?!"She recieved a sharp look as a couple passed."I have important matters. Don't worry. Just keep your head down."And with that, they parted.

It was three hours later that Kripin pulled aside Charles. He'd been speaking to the daughter of the mayor of a nearby city, acting as any nobleman would, and didn't even notice his second in command before he tugged on his suit. He looked as discreet and respectful as any butler would. Charles excused himself from the conversation with the rich folk and lowered his head as Kripin gave him a severe look."I can't find Maria," he whispered. "I lost her.""You lost her," Charles repeated, keeping his voice restrained but his tone sharp."She just disappeared in the crowd. I've been looking for the past hour."Charles noted the faint smell of sweat and Kripin's flushed cheeks to support his story. He raised his gaze, tried to find the unmistakeable red curls.He immediately did. And they were rushing towards him."Charles!" Maria yelled. When that earned her looks she lowered her voice to a conspicous whisper and repeated, "Charles!"He grabbed her as she almost tripped on the last step to him. He noted her bloodshot eyes."Maria," he said with a dangerous tone. "Are you drunk?""Good news," she slurred. "I found the kitchen staff's quarters! They have some delicious stuff there. Herbs and whatnot.""Drugs."Kripin and Charles shared a severe look."D on't be mad, I did what you said!"Charles gripped her upper arms harder, earning a dazed grin. He looked ready to shake her senseless."I didn't tell you to get high.""No, you told me to find Gooden. And I did. He's right," she turned around, closed one eye and pointed across the crowd with a finger wavering as if it weighed a hundred pounds, "there.""This isn't good, boss. We can't leave her like this.""But we can't face Gooden just one of us. It's too risky."They both gave the high Maria disdained looks. Then eachother."We'll have to bring her."

A/nHeyyyoPlease be proud of me that I finally finished this chapter with everything going on

Chapter Fifteen

S ecretS

Charles had been worried about Maria's presence during the confrontation with mayor Gooden but it soon became a non-issue. By the time the three were ascending the grande staircase, following Gooden at a reasonable distance into a more secluded area of the manor, she'd lost conciousness.Charles would be worried was it not for the faint snoring sounding at the back of her throat. Instead of waking her up he decided just to grab an arm and a leg and carry her the rest of the way.

Unconcious, she was much less of a hassle -- though heavier than she looked -- and Charles and Kripin had soon fallen into a predatory thoughtlessness. They stopped behind a corner just as mayor Gooden disappeared into an office further down the corridor."This is it," Kripin mumbled, his eyes undertaking an excited, yellow hue. "He's gonna be alone.""But we won't," Charles retorted, referring to the dozed off human in his arms."W e'll leave her here.""No. If anyone sees her we're done.""Oh, come on. The worst they'll do is take her."Silence."Oh.""It's not an option, Kripin.""With all due respect, it's the only one there is. What are you suggesting we do? Bring her?"

Mayor Gooden jumped as the door to the office slammed open. Waltzing in came a lean, suited fellow. His appearance was impeccable, yet a poorly stored away maliciousness tugged at the corner of his lips. Gooden grabbed the armrests on his chair but paused in the last second, wondering if it wasn't safer keeping the large desk between him and the stranger.Another man entered not too far behind. He was large and intimidating but what really made Gooden's face an alarming shade of red was the girl in his arms. She was done up, painted, but he recognized her.This time he couldn't keep up the facade."Well, hello there.""I don't know you! Who let you up here?"They moved closer."Get that thing away from me!" he squealed, his voice a strange pitch, pointing to Maria.Kripin and Charles shared a look -- maybe their claws wouldn't be necessary to scare the man, it seems Maria had done the job.Charles let Maria fall into one of the plush armchairs stuffed alongside the walls, the expensive fabric waiting for politicians and benefactors, and got up alongside Kripin, crossing his arms."Let's get to the point, Gooden. We know who you are, and we don't have any quarrel with you."His eyes were still on Maria."We do advice you to contain your civilian troop, though.""The civilian troop?"Kripin moved around the table swiftly, barely making a sound, and planted an arm around the back of Gooden's chair."Yes," he said lowly. "They're getting a little too close, don't you think?""I-I do.""And they have taken too much of the town's funds to be chasing wild goose?""Absolutely!""I'm glad we're on the same page."He planted a hand on Gooden's shoulder, making the old man jump, and allowed his claws to extend. Just a bit. Then he returned to Charles' side, crossed his arms. Gooden looked like he'd drop dead any second. And that was that. At least it should have been.

"Why do you hate her so much?"Kripin and Gooden gave Charles the same look. Both also remained quiet for well over five seconds."Boss, we have what we came for.""Silence, Kripin. Gooden, tell me.""How could I not, she's--"Charles' seemed to become twice as big suddenly, making Gooden rethink his words. His eyes traveled to her."You have no idea what she's done, what she is.""She's done nothing but be alive. She's your people and you're despicable for allowing the abuse you have.""So that's what she's told you?" he stopped Charles halfway through turning back to the door.Heartbeats. Four of them, all in the same strained rhytm for a second. Everyone looks to Maria."What do you mean?""Charles," Kripin warns. His eyes hold a silent plea. But it's too late."She killed her brother."

×A/NIt's short but I can't procrastinate anymore. Tell me off in the comments so I'm not allowed to leave for 20 days again lol

Chapter Sixteen

L ieS

The room was way too cold. The light streaming in through the windows was blue and harsh, clearly from the moon, and caught stray dust particles as they wafted through the air. Undisturbed. Dead.Maria raised her head."Hello?"She looked down at her hands pressed against the mattress and then felt the familiar sheets as she wiggled her toes. She was back in her room in the Den. Not for all the pennies in the world could she figure out why.

It wasn't long until something began nagging her. Even as she laid her head back on the pillow, feeling drained, the thought wouldn't allow her to sleep. Neither did her bladder.Trying not to think too much about it, Maria forced herself to swing her feet over the edge of the bed and then, wobbly and disoriented, blindly stagger to the door. She knew the bathroom was five metres ahead, the third of four doors. Her body mindlessly brought her forward. Maria reached for the handle. Opened. It took a few seconds for her to realize she'd opened the wrong door. Then another five to process what she was looking at.

The room looked like something out of a conspiracy theorist's lair. Papers were everywhere, stacked on the floor forming huge piles, photos too hard to make out in the dark were pinned to the wall along with red thread and in the middle was a small desk. On top it sat an empty mug and a thin, brown file.

Maria knew she'd probably walked into something she wasn't supposed to know existed, but that instantly made it all that more allouring. She looked behind her, hearing the rest of the Den completely silent, and then took a step forward. Then another one. Her careful steps had soon brought her to the far-end wall and she squinted at one of the photos pinned to it. Attached was a thread leading somewhere else, perhaps to another photo.It was a man. No older than herself but with a look in his eye as if he'd aged tenfold. He was looking into the camera, his face sunken in and tinted blue. The photo brought chills down her spine. Underneath was a note attached by tape with a word scribbled in black ink: "Threat?"

She put her index finger to the thread and moved away from the photo. It was a bit too haunting for her taste and in the darkness she could almost feel the man's eyes following her. Her naked toes stiffened against the cold floor but she didn't dare start a fire, too scared of getting caught.Maria followed the thread to another photograph, this one so blurry that she had to move a glowing fingertip up against it to see properly. It was the same man but not beaten and bruised, this time accompanied by a woman. They were kissing. Around them were tall houses and streetlamps illuminating the night. The photo seemed taken from afar, the person holding the camera hidden behind something as if not wanting to be seen. Maria's finger lingered on the couple and she almost got lost at the sight of such tenderness. Then she noticed the note underneath, this one not as vague: "There are two of them."

Once again, Maria followed the attached thread. She walked past the room's window then a vase just barely avoided by her reaching steps, and then stopped. Her fingers moved to this photo as well.

This photo was taken outside a window. The night was incredibly dark but from the window came a warm hue. It was Christmas -- Maria could tell because a Christmas tree had been put up inside the house. Around it was a family: two men and five women, some drinking and some having a laugh. Kids were scattered around them, babies and teenagers.Maria's eyes shot open; a gasp passed her lips. Closest to the window was a woman holding a candle. The tip of her index finger was burning.

Maria's breath was gone by that point but her eyes still moved down to the attached note. This one was simple, but invited a stampede into Maria's mind: "Thousands."

She backed away. The thread continued but she couldn't bring herself to look. Something hit against the back of her knees and she quickly put her hand down to steady herself. Maria felt the thick paper against her fingertips and had identified it before she could think straight -- the file."Please," she murmured to herself as she turned around, grabbed the file in her hands. "Please no."She let it fall open.Her own face looked back at her.The photo had been taken when she was sleeping. A soft stream of black smoke ringled past her parted lips before dissipating into the air. Her hair was messy and big but had been moved as to not cover her face.

Empathetic, Loud, Emotional

The words were written beside her photo.

Spy?

Maria felt him before he made himself known. A rough hand grabbed her arm and pulled her back and before she could think to fight she was back in front of her door. Charles now towered over her. His glare was sharp.

Dangerous."WHAT MADE YOU THINK THAT WAS OKAY?!""There are thousands like me," Maria said, more to herself than him. "Truly thousands?""Maria..." he warned, chest heaving. "Get back in your room. Now.""You've known for a while.""Of course I have," he snapped. "I know every possible threat to my pack.""But you knew how long I've been wondering what I am... You knew how lonely I felt."He didn't respond. Maria decided to ask something else."What did you do to him, Charles? The man in the photograph. Did you torture him? Who is he?""A possible threat.""Like me."He suddenly looked pained."They came too close a few years back and I had them... investigated. But they never attacked, that particular family lives in New York last I checked."Family. The word hurt more than she cared to admit to him."You have a file on me. Am I going to end up like him?""Don't be ridiculous!""YOU'VE LIED TO ME!"

The cold air sparked as Charles' shoulders dropped. He leant back. Crossed his arms. His face closed, Maria saw it happen."You want to talk about lies... You didn't tell me you killed your brother."Maria felt her heart stop."How do you know?""In the same way you do. I wasn't going to say anything but how can you possibly blame me for fearing you in the beginning?" Charles said, his voice softened. "You clearly were."

Maria grabbed his shoulder, pushed him aside, and walked past him. Her steps aimed for the stairs but she couldn't tell if she was on track since her eyes were blurry with tears. Charles didn't call after her but a hand engulfed her lower arm, forcing her to momentarily stop."Please," the softest voice she imagined he could conjur pleaded. "Not like this."She tore away."What was it again? Emotional? Loud? A threat?""Maria--""I killed my brother. Don't think I won't kill you too." Her hands were instantly engulfed by flames, making his cower away. "This has been nice, and I thank you for your help," her montone voice offered. It was the one suited for the monster everyone seemed to think she was. "But I think I've overstayed my welcome."

Charles didn't follow her as Maria stormed down the staircase. She tried to tell herself that was a good thing. She tried not to tremble too much as her fingers enveloped the handle of the front door.

Outside was lonely and silent but Maria reckoned she would have to get used to it. Or maybe not.

New York.

Charles' own truck was hard to miss. It stood idle by the treeline, a bit scrappy but that only made it easier to steal. It seemed it had been wired by the pack before and it took no more than five minutes to figure out how to get it started but as she drove off she didn't dare look behind her in fear of seeing a giant, angry monster. No -- she didn't want that, she reminded herself.

As she made it a bit ways into the forest, her shoulders sunk and her emotions got the upper hand. For the first time in forever, tears streamed down her cheeks. At first just the one. Then more than she'd ever allowed herself to experience. Her hands shook, making the driving uneven, but she kept on track.

She had stolen a car and she would drive for as long as she could. Hopefully she'd end up on the other side of the world before getting tired -- or just New York. The thought was calming and without thinking too much about it, she let her foot press down harder on the gaspedal.

Charles watched her drive off. He felt the warmth leave alongside her. He told himself that was a good thing. Now he had a potential threat, along with any problems accompanying her, gone. It was a good thing.But he couldn't convince himself she truly was a spy, nor dangerous. His hands morphed, his bones itched to chase.He decided to move away from the window."Kripin?"The familiar feeling of a joint mind came to him, telling he was being heard. Charles closed his eyes."Maria is no longer with us."

It took a minute before Kripin came bursting into Charles' office. By then he saw his boss sitting calmly behind his desk, raising an eyebrow."I didn't tell you to come.""She's gone?"His eyes went back to what ever could be more important laying on his desk."Yes.""With all due respect, boss, are you crazy?""Kripin," he warned. "I'm not in the mood to be tested. And why do you care? Why should I? She's been nothing but trouble, danger, and she interrupted my spiritual journey." At this point he was standing. "She took away an invaluable reward that journey was to grant me!"Kripin didn't look scared. For the first time he didn't read his superior's mood and act accordingly. Instead he ran a stressed hand through his hair. His voice was trembling with kept emotion."Once again, are you insane?"Nothing. Which only seemed to make Kripin even more frustrated. He broke."SHE WAS THE REWARD!" A harsh breath. "Anyone could see it, boss. She made you better. Granted, she was a pain, but the universe gave her to you and you--""Threw her out."Charles looked stressed now as well. But a gleam of joy showed in his eyes. He thought Kripin didn't notice. He did."We have to get her.""Yes, boss," he breathed, relieved. "You really do."

×A/n

Would you look at that? The book is done. Ended on a cliffhanger (I'm a psycho, I know) but you can imagine your own ending.

Hope you enjoyed reading! I for sure enjoyed writing for you all.

See you soon! Keep your eyes out for a new story.

Chapter Seventeen

EndinG

Maria wasn't often cold - but that night her skin was prickly and sore. The night loomed; the mighty trees stood back and watched as the feral cold bit onto her cheeks. She thought about warming herself but each time she began reaching for the small ball of burning within her, the word "Spy?" popped up in her head. So did others: New York. Did her fate truly lie there? Or had Charles lied to her? Charles - another word she could not seem to shake.

He lied, her mind hissed time and time again. He lied and he would not hesitate to do it again, you dirty little killer.

Maria's foot got lodged in a hidden root. She flailed but to no avail. The ground was even more merciless on her body than the air. She stayed lying.

Killer, the voice spat again. Nasty little murderer. That is what you do. You kill. You destroy. You're dangerous.

Dangerous!

Dangerous!

Dangerous!

"Fuck off!" Her hand slammed into the ground. A wave of warmth surged through the hardened earth surrounding her, making it into slimey soil. Her body sunk into it. Yet she couldn't bring herself up. "I'm not a killer."

She didn't expect the forest to respond.

"I know."

The wolf looked down at her, his face as indecipherable as ever as the moon only found its way to his eyes. They gleamed. He reached forward a hand.

"Maria," Charles said and put his palm closer. "Get up.""Get the fuck away." She not-so-gracefully got to her knees. From there she quickly jumped to her feet. "Don't even look at me.""Maria," he began, but his eyes did move down to her muddied clothes and bare feet. "I need to speak to you. But not here. Please-""You changed your mind, huh? You decided to kill me after all." Her eyes were flaming in every way except literal. It was clear she had no fuel left to light.

Before Charles could even respond, Maria charged. She got less than a fingertip's distance away. Then she stopped. Just as Charles thought he was definitely getting killed, perished in a fiery death, she closed her eyes."Do it then. I can't fight back so do it. But don't fucking look me in the eyes when you do.""Maria-""Be quiet." Her voice became snow; soft, gentle snow instead of sparking flames. Her head angled upward. "I don't want my last moment to be words."Charles' face was darker than ever. He was grateful she could not see his hands morph between human ones and feral, livid claws. "You truly think I came here to kill you?""I killed my brother, fair is fair, right? You may hate me.""It was an accident.""Don't tell my story for me. No, it wasn't. I burnt the house down, I knew he was in there." Her mouth remained open for a second, her shut eyes twitched a little bit. "It was the only self-defence I had left after he broke my hands."

Silence.

Maria wondered how death would be like. She had avoided it multiple times, ran from it even, but never imagined it. And now, it had found her in the form of Charles. Charles. She found herself listening for chirping birds even in the night, and hoping that death felt a little bit like her time with Charles. Like burnt meat, safety - comfort.

Two palms slowly came upon her cheeks. They were so warm it made her eyelids flicker open for just a second. She saw Charles eyes were closed as well as he moved his hands to rest by her jaw. She felt a tear disintegrate on her lips, the salt spread across her tongue.

She shut her eyes harder as the grip tightened.

"Not once have I hated you."

Soft, soft lips. They slowly graced hers. At first, she thought they were feathers. Then, as he breathed into her, she thought it was death. Her eyes fluttered open, eyelashes clumped by tears. Charles was close, closer than she'd thought - his lips were still feathery on hers.

"Please," he whispered, "forgive me. If you don't... I do not know what to do."

Maria felt how her body had gone limp, the fear of death draining along with any and all energy, and Charles was practically holding her up by her cheeks. She swallowed. Hard. Yet no words came out.

"Forgive me," he said again, this time not even daring to look in her eyes. "Forgive me, forgive me. Please. I need you, in any way I may have you. Don't leave, please do not leave.""You mean...?"He nodded, still close to her lips.Maria said the only thing she could think of. "Are there truly more of me in New York?""Yes. I know where." Charles tried to collect himself. It was clear she could not forgive him. Although it made his instincts so conflicted that a sharp pain shot through his head, he backed away. Just one step.

They looked at each other.

"We have a lot to talk about," she trailed, her voice just as frail as his. She harshly wiped a tear from her cheek, leaving it red."We do." Charles ran a hand through his hair, heard how his breath trembled as he exhaled. "But you deserve to know the truth. I will help you find it. If you even wish for my help any longer, that is. We'll go to New York and--"

Maria's arms landed perfectly across his shoulders. Her lips smashed onto his, not feather-light as his had been but instead vibrating with energy. Her hair sparked like fireworks in the dark woods. She moved to get closer but before she knew it, Charles had brought her into his arms.Maria placed a hand on his chest, pulled back a little. "I'm sorry I didn't tell you--"The growl rising from Charles' throat didn't leave room for apologies. He pulled her closer, his hands strong yet the most careful pair that had ever touched her. She felt the claws tease her skin."You truly believe I deserve a family?" she asked, breathless as he let her part just an inch.He nodded. His eyes were darker than ever, so deep that the night seemed more safe. Yet she got closer."Please, return with me to the Den.""I can't."Charles' face fell. His grip loosened. "Why not?"Maria felt how his his heart quickened against hers. She noticed once again how sharp and rugged his features were while somehow suiting well together. Even riled up, he seemed in control of most things. She patted a small spot where her hair had caught on fire and pulled a few strands behind her ear.

"Because your jacket sleeve is burning."

××

A/N

Here! I hope I did it justice. Either way, I really was happy to write out a better ending. To write at all, actually, for the first time in many months.

Thank you once again, I can't believe more than 100 people have read the book.

I wrote this quickly because I got such a surge of inspiration and didn't want to waste it. I apologize for any errors.

I love you!